Halloween

Illustrated by Donald Grant
and Pierre-Marie Valat
Written by Jacqueline Vallon
Created by Gallimard Jeunesse

MOONLIGHT PUBLISHING / FIRST DISCOVERY

On the 31st of October every year,
as soon as darkness falls, strange figures begin
to appear and go
up and down
the streets.

It's **HALLOWEEN!**

In Britain, Ireland, America, Canada and now more and more countries, children - and grown-ups too - try to come up with their best disguises as witches, vampires and other scary creatures, which haunt our bad dreams.

Children go knocking at the doors of their neighbours and friends and ask: « Trick or treat? »

Better to give
them sweets,
fruit or nuts...
or anything
can happen:
your door
covered in jam,
or your cat
painted green...

It is an ancient custom, which dates back over 2000 years !
The Celts used to celebrate that night as they entered a new year. Spirits rose up then after dark and mixed with the people.

Christians also celebrate 1st November as All Saints' Day and the 2nd as All Souls' Day.

st November, Samhain's Day,
marked the end of summer
and the beginning of
the cold season

Big fires were lit in honour
of the sun, so that it would
return to full strength
after winter.

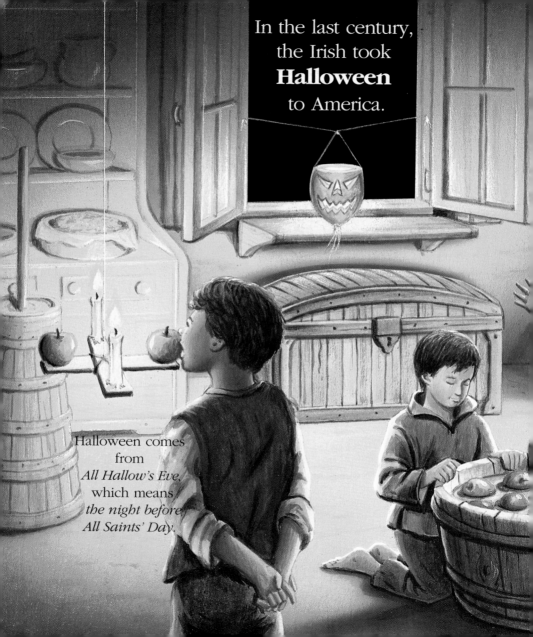

In the last century,
the Irish took
Halloween
to America.

Halloween comes
from
All Hallow's Eve,
which means
the night before
All Saints' Day.

In Ireland the doors were left open to welcome the souls of the dead. A seat by the fire and food were kept for them. The customary meal was *calcannon,* boiled cabbage and *barmbrack,* a currant bun.

One of the traditional games was "ducking for apples". No hands allowed!

It is the night
of the spirits ...

Ghosts, witches,
goblins, fairies and vampires...
All the creatures, who inhabit
the invisible world,
come out.

And let's not forget their trusty companions:
owls, toads, spiders, black cats and bats...

Where did the idea of the pumpkin lantern come from?

It is an Irish tradition and goes back to the tale of a man called Jack, who sold his soul to the devil. When he died, he was condemned to wander for ever after in neverending darkness.

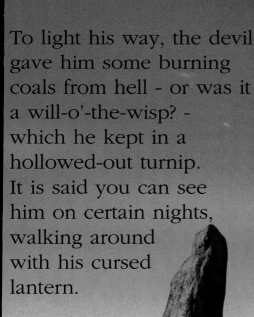

To light his way, the devil
gave him some burning
coals from hell - or was it
a will-o'-the-wisp? -
which he kept in a
hollowed-out turnip.
It is said you can see
him on certain nights,
walking around
with his cursed
lantern.

On Halloween night,
it has become the custom to make lanterns
by hollowing out a turnip or a beet or even a lerge
potato to conjure up the image of the dead souls,
who wander the earth on that night.
In America it is a pumpkin that has become *Jack's lantern* .

How to make a pumkin lantern?

Choose a round pumpkin. Cut a lid off the top.

Spoon out the inside of the pumpkin, leaving just the sides about 3 cm thick. (Be very careful not to go through them!)

Draw eyes, a nose and a mouth on the pumpkin, and then cut them out with a sharp knife. Pour some candlewax into the pumpkin and fix a candle in it. Light it and put the lid back on the pumpkin. Now place the lantern in a dark corner…Ahhh!

The more scary they are,
the better !

You can also add hair, a beard and teeth with the help of twigs, dried fruit, vegetable stalks, and raffia etc.

Halloween Soup!
Boil the flesh of the pumpkin
you have spooned out and add
salt, pepper and sugar. Then put it all
through the mixer. add some fresh cream and
a few croutons. What a feast!

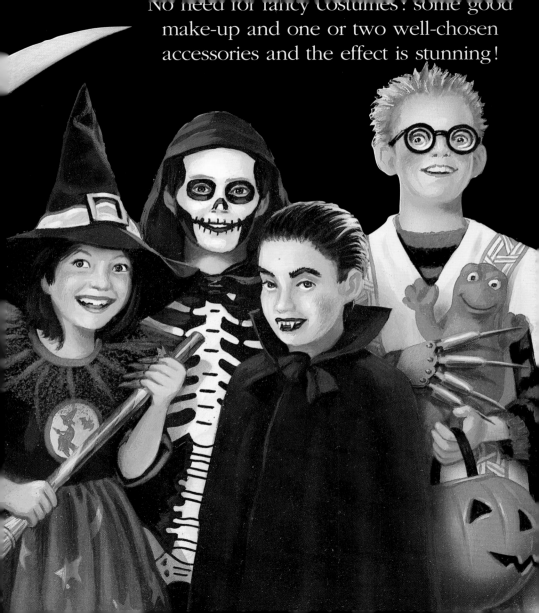

No need for fancy costumes! Some good make-up and one or two well-chosen accessories and the effect is stunning!

Create a nightmare scenario

To make these decorations, draw a pattern of faces or ghosts on a roll of paper; fold it like an accordeon and cut it out .

Candles, cobwebs, paper chains, mobiles
and balloons painted with grimacing faces…

Put lanterns in the corners of the room; don't forget background noises of hooting,

clanking, scraping and rustling, diabolical laughter, groaning and sighing…

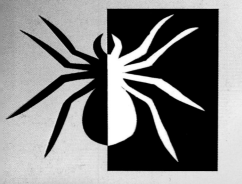

Now everything is ready for
some party games
Here are a few ideas…

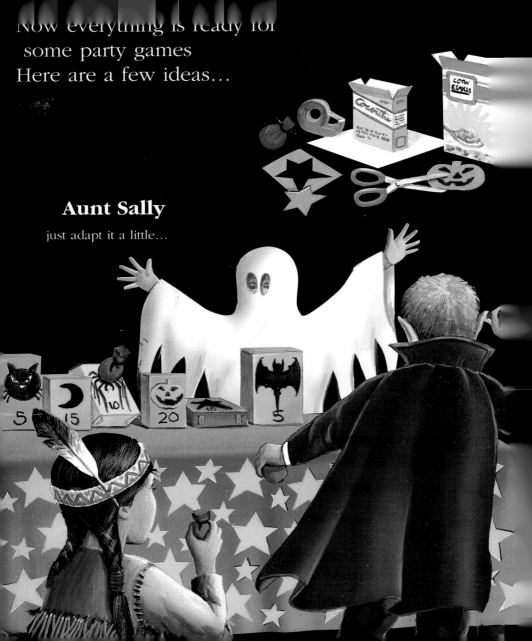

Aunt Sally

just adapt it a little…

The box of horrors

If you want to get the sweeties, you have to put your hand through a thick layer of horrible, slimy stuff...

Cold spaghetti feels just like snakes,

wet grapes make you think of eyes torn from their sockets,

cold cooked rice could easily be maggots...

Ducking for apples: **the traditional game**.

The devil's pizza

Tomato sauce,
sweet corn

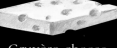
Gruyère cheese,
sausage

Ham,
hard-boiled eggs...

Carrots and olives

The death cake

Draw a skull on a sponge cake with icing sugar. Fill the rest with chocolate.

The simplest cake can become the devil's delight!

FIRST DISCOVERY: OVER 100 TITLES AVAILABLE IN FOUR SERIES

AMERICAN INDIANS
ANIMAL CAMOUFLAGE
BABIES
BEARS
THE BEAVER
THE BEE
BEING BORN
BIRDS
BOATS
THE BODY
THE BUILDING SITE
THE BUTTERFLY
THE CASTLE
CATHEDRALS
CATS
CHRISTMAS AND NEW YEAR
CLOTHES AND COSTUMES
COLOURS
COUNTING
THE DESERT
DINOSAURS
DOGS
DUCKS
THE EAGLE
EARTH AND SKY
THE EGG
THE ELEPHANT
FARM ANIMALS
FINDING A MATE
FIREFIGHTING
FLOWERS
FLYING
FOOTBALL
THE FROG
FRUIT
GROWING UP
HALLOWEEN
HANDS, FEET AND PAWS

THE HORSE
HOW THE BODY WORKS
THE INTERNET
THE JUNGLE
THE LADYBIRD
LIGHT
THE LION
MONKEYS AND APES
MOUNTAINS
THE MOUSE
MUSIC
ON WHEELS
THE OWL
PENGUINS
PICTURES
PREHISTORIC PEOPLE
PYRAMIDS
RABBITS
THE RIVERBANK
THE SEASHORE
SHAPES
SHOPS
SMALL ANIMALS IN THE HOME
SPORT
THE STORY OF BREAD
THE TELEPHONE
TIME
THE TOOLBOX
TOWN
TRAINS
THE TREE
UNDER THE GROUND
UP AND DOWN
VEGETABLES
WATER
THE WEATHER
WHALES
THE WOLF

FIRST DISCOVERY / ATLAS

ANIMAL ATLAS
ATLAS OF ANIMALS IN DANGER
ATLAS OF CIVILIZATIONS
ATLAS OF COUNTRIES
ATLAS OF THE EARTH
ATLAS OF FRANCE
ATLAS OF ISLANDS
ATLAS OF PEOPLES
ATLAS OF SPACE
PLANT ATLAS

FIRST DISCOVERY / ART

ANIMALS
HENRI MATISSE
THE IMPRESSIONISTS
LANDSCAPES
THE LOUVRE
PABLO PICASSO
PAINTINGS
PORTRAITS
SCULPTURE
VINCENT VAN GOGH

FIRST DISCOVERY / TORCHLIGHT

LET'S LOOK AT ANIMALS BY NIGHT
LET'S LOOK AT ANIMALS UNDERGROUND
LET'S LOOK AT ARCHIMBOLDO'S PORTRAITS
LET'S LOOK AT CASTLES
LET'S LOOK AT CAVES
LET'S LOOK AT DINOSAURS
LET'S LOOK AT FISH UNDERWATER
LET'S LOOK AT LIFE BELOW THE CITY
LET'S LOOK AT INSECTS
LET'S LOOK AT THE SKY
LET'S LOOK FOR LOST TREASURE
LET'S LOOK INSIDE THE BODY
LET'S LOOK INSIDE PYRAMIDS

r, East Hendred, Oxon. OX12 8JY